GHOSTS REVISITED 5

![cover image of dolls]

William P. Robertson

The tales in this book come from local folklore, friends' testimonies, and internet research. They are as factual as the author could make them although other versions are sometimes told.

Published by BookBaby
www.bookbaby.com

CONTENTS

CREDITS

Many thanks to the "Birdman," Bob Burns, for the stark hawk and crow photos he contributed. The scaffold photograph on page 12 is courtesy of the Jefferson County History Center. The Congelier House photo has appeared in numerous online articles and podcasts and is in the public domain.

The creepy dolls are courtesy of the Salamanca Antique Mall in Salamanca, NY. The Duffy's Historic Boalsburg Tavern postcard was printed by Whitman's Phototypes in Canton, PA and dates back to the 1950s. The Belhurst Castle postcard is a product of Bill Bard Associates, Inc., Monticello, NY. The Sullivan Brothers photo comes from the Library of Congress.

The "Green Man of Pittsburgh" pics were provided by Ryan Cavalline of Legend Hunters Films. A more detailed version of the Green Man tale is covered in Ryan's movie, *Myths and Mutants*. The owl photos are by Susie Coffman. All other photographs are by William P. Robertson.

Author, Eric Armstrong, provided helpful information for the "Jefferson County Courthouse" story. David Crowley, meanwhile, shared his knowledge about historic people buried in the Cuba, NY cemetery.

A big "thank you" goes out to owner, Todd Hennard, for his cooperation during the writing of the "Beefeaters" story.

Marcie Schellhammer, assistant managing editor of the *Bradford Era*, furnished the account of her mother's Bigfoot sighting in Westline, PA that served as a basis for the tale on page 43.

Iroquois Supernatural by Michael Bastine and Mason Winfield is a great source of information about Native American legends.

Another version of "Hunting in a Haunted Forest" first appeared in the Saturday, December 3, 2022 issue of the *Bradford Era*, Bradford, PA.

Thanks also to artist, David Cox, for creating the eerie cover. David may be contacted at dlcox1972@gmail.com.

CUBA CEMETERY

The cemetery in Cuba, New York sits on a hilltop overlooking Medbury Road. It was established in 1841 when two acres of land were purchased from Lewis Nash. At first, the Catholic and Protestant graveyards were separated by a tall, board fence, so the Protestants wouldn't have to view the Irish tombstones. The fence was finally taken down in 1923. 2015 is another significant date in the cemetery's history. In that year, it was added to the National Register of Historic Places by the United States Department of the Interior.

The Cuba Cemetery is home to many illustrious soldiers. Ashbel Webster, for example, was a Revolutionary War hero who fought at the

Battles of Bunker Hill and Long Island. There are also two Medal of Honor winners from the Civil War. L. Franklin Packard rescued a comrade from three Rebels while serving with the 5th New York Cavalry. Harlan Swift, meanwhile, single-handedly captured four enemy infantrymen during the Siege of Petersburg.

The graveyard contains two interesting buildings, as well. One was built in 1914 and served as a receiving vault. Bodies were kept there during frigid winters when the ground was too frozen to dig graves. The other structure is the McKee Mausoleum that was erected in 1875 when the family's daughter, Josephine, died suddenly at the age of twenty-one. Resembling an oversized dollhouse, the tomb was furnished with Victorian era chairs and side tables along with portraits of Josephine and her parents. Much of the furniture is no longer there.

In the 1970s, Cuba Cemetery was having a problem with vandals. David Crowley, president of the Cemetery Association, volunteered to patrol the graveyard from dusk until midnight to collar any trespassers. Darting shadows and flashes of light kept him on edge during his watch. Reflections of headlights from nearby Route 305 were spooky, too, when they glanced off polished tombstones. He also heard the weird calls of night birds and other unidentified creatures. Crowley gave up his vigil after just a few nights before he caught defacers not made of flesh and blood!

JEFFERSON COUNTY COURTHOUSE

Located in Brookville, Pennsylvania, the original Jefferson County Courthouse was built in 1832 by John Lucas and Thomas Barr. A two-story stone jailhouse was erected a year earlier behind it. By 1866, a new "temple of justice" was needed, and James T. Dickey began its construction on May 30th. It took three long years to finish the project. Court was conducted in the Presbyterian Church in the meantime.

Between 1867 and 1905, public executions were held behind the old jail or on the lawn between the courthouse and jail. In all, four men were hung for murder. The first, Charles Chase, was convicted of cracking Elizabeth McDonald's

11

skull with a wood maul while robbing her. The other killers were Italian mine or construction workers. They included Michael Pallone, Thomas Aiello, and Francesco Cefoli. Cefoli, in particular, swore he was innocent even as the noose was threaded around his neck. Evidence clearly showed, though, that he shot a fellow worker five times in cold blood and intended to use the slain man's savings to return to Italy.

Since these executions, a west wing was added to the Jefferson County Courthouse where the dreaded scaffold once stood. This is also the site of several hauntings witnessed by a dispatcher who worked in the basement there. One night, while manning the phones in the 911 Call Center, he heard a typewriter clacking madly in the next room. He had been alone all evening, so he left his station to investigate.

The hair stood up on the dispatcher's neck when he discovered said typewriter lying on the floor. He immediately called the police to comb the building. They arrived moments later only to find the Smith Corona back on the table where it belonged. Had Cefoli's ghost been punching the keys? To express his considerable anger?

Larry Anthony is postmaster of Brookville and heads the local paranormal group. He's also documented spooky activity at the courthouse. According to Larry, footsteps and noises are heard frequently by nighttime attendants. Doors have opened and closed on their own, as well, and chairs scrape across the floor by themselves in the Register and Recorder Office. Orbs have been spotted in the main courtroom, too, as miscreant spirits roam about the building playing pranks or protesting the "justice" they received.

ATTUNED

Some people are ghost magnets. Tom Seagren is one of them. Until he retired, Tom designed lighters for Zippo Manufacturing in Bradford, Pennsylvania. His artistic sensibilities made him attuned to the supernatural, as well.

When Tom was a teenager, he lived in an old, rambling house on West Washington Street. The Sunday before Halloween, his parents went shopping to Jamestown, New York. After much pleading, he was allowed to stay home and play football with his neighborhood pals. In the 1960s, kids would rather tackle and crunch each other than watch the sport on television.

That day, their game got so intense, it raged until dark. After exchanging insults with the opposing team, Tom stomped off down the street. With a sigh, he mounted his porch steps, exhausted and covered with mud. He was greeted at the door by his tail-wagging dog. Together, they headed for the bathroom on the second floor.

Tom had just begun climbing the stairs when his dog emitted a warning growl. All of its hair stood up on end as the cloudy figure of a man appeared from nowhere and hovered eerily in the air above them. Tom didn't wait for it to float nearer. He let out a shriek and bolted from the house, forgetting all about his bruised muscles. Yipping wildly, his dog fled, too.

Seagren shivered in the front yard until his parents came home an hour later. After he told them what he had seen, his father said, "The Jews who owned this house before us survived the Holocaust. They are now all dead. The dad was especially brutalized. He must have sympathized with how battered you look and appeared to console you."

"But he scared the heck out of me!" yelped Tom. "I hope he 'comforts' someone else next time."

Years later, Tom bought a home on Congress Street from Tony Muto's widow. When he went to pick up the keys, he gave her his drawing of the beautiful brick mansion she had inhabited for over forty years. She burst into tears upon seeing it, for she had spent her entire married life there. Mrs. Muto left Bradford soon after to live with her daughter in Florida.

Tom and his family moved into 141 Congress Street, and a peaceful decade passed. One balmy afternoon, he fell asleep while watching TV. His wife and daughters had left to visit relatives, and he was alone in the house. He dozed for some time before a particularly loud commercial jarred him awake. Startled, he opened his eyes and found himself staring at the misty apparition of a familiar-looking lady. She vanished in an instant—before he could recognize her face.

It wasn't until the next morning that Tom realized Mrs. Muto had paid him a visit. She had stopped to say goodbye to her beloved home and to the artist who drew a cherish picture of it. He knew it was Mrs. M. after reading her obituary in the *Bradford Era*. . .

DUFFY'S TAVERN

Duffy's Tavern is located in Boalsburg, Pennsylvania on Route 45 near State College. Built in 1819 at the crossroads of two stagecoach routes, it was originally called Springfield Tavern. The establishment burned on Valentine's Day of 1934. It was rebuilt and then sold to Harry Duffy who gave it its current name. Duffy died in the foyer in 1961 and is now one of four ghosts that haunt the premises.

A young woman is also seen in the dining room wearing a yellow dress. Many mistake her for a waitress until she vanishes while taking their order. The specter, Michael, though, is just four years old and stays in the Gold Room. He's been known to appear to those who call his name and offer him a stuffed animal. The other phantom stomps about the second floor in a heavy pair of boots and likes to warm himself by the upstairs fireplace. This soldier from the Civil War has established himself as the dominant male entity.

Diners who frequent Duffy's Tavern often see tables move by themselves, hear the clinking of glasses, and watch pepper shakers topple over. Tracey Moriarty, the current co-owner, hears the slamming of office doors at all hours of the day. She's also spied a wispy woman walking on the porch.

Several paranormal teams have performed investigations at the restaurant, as well. One group filmed an orb that descended the stairs, bobbed into two rooms, and then floated back up the staircase. They also found the vacant apartment on the third floor haunted. Voices were recorded by their Phasmabox there, and knocks were returned by responsive spirits.

Tracey has had eerie experiences on the top floor, too. While she was watching, a window was shoved open, knocking down the box that held it shut. Then a second window opened on its own no matter how many times she locked it.

20 SCHOOL STREET

The Gothic brick manor at 20 School Street in Bradford, Pennsylvania has a long history of unique tenants. For years, it served as a funeral home before becoming the office of the Visiting Nurse Association.

When the VNA occupied the building, rumors surfaced about it being haunted. Objects reputedly appeared from nowhere while doors slammed shut for no reason. One nurse refused a job after a half-hour interview because of the spooky activity she witnessed. Then a cleaning lady swore she heard party noises upstairs. The merriment stopped, however, when her duties took her to the top floor.

Now, a reclusive psychiatrist lives there who immediately took steps to insure his privacy. First, he installed a stout iron gate across the driveway. He also planted a row of pines to hide his residence from view. No house number is on display, either, to further discourage intruders.

It's a good thing, though, that a shrink moved into the creepy, old mansion. From eyewitness accounts of the place, it's believed that its ghosts are in need of serious counseling!

CONGELIER HOUSE

Charles Congelier made his fortune rebuilding the South after the Civil War had destroyed much of it. In the late 1860s, he then moved to Pittsburgh, Pennsylvania where he erected a luxurious mansion for himself; his wife, Lyda; and their maid, Essie. The manor was located at 1129 Ridge Avenue in the Manchester neighborhood on the Northside. It soon became known as "the house the devil built" because of the evil that occurred there.

After moving into their new home, Congelier began a torrid affair with his lusty maid. His wife caught them in the throes of passion and went berserk. Grabbing a meat cleaver from the kitchen, she hacked the lovers into little pieces as she raved and cursed at them. Neighbors found her a few days later calmly swaying in her rocking chair. She was humming lullabies to Essie's severed head that was cradled in her arms like a bloody child.

The home sat vacant for two decades due to this horrific murder that shocked the entire city. Finally, in 1892, a railroad company bought it to divide into apartments for its workers. Immediately, the men were plagued by demons that prowled the halls and shrieked at them from dark corners. Even the tough Irish couldn't stand such torment, and the railroad put the place back on the market.

The next owner purchased the property in 1900. He was a German-born doctor named Adolph C. Brunrichter and the quietest neighbor ever. That was until the night of August 12, 1901 when a woman's screams emitted from the bowels of his house. It wasn't until strange lights burst from the windows that the police were summoned. When the officers arrived, a decapitated woman was lying in the hall squirting blood from her torso. A lab was soon discovered in the basement along with five more women's heads. Although the doctor had disappeared, his notes were spotted near a gory operating table. They explained in graphic detail his attempts to keep the severed heads alive.

The next tenants at 1129 Ridge Avenue had similar horrors awaiting them. The Equitable Gas Company converted the home into a dormitory for its immigrant workers who immediately learned they weren't alone. They complained of shadows that walked through walls until two of their fellows were found dead in the basement. Although they'd been murdered, no suspects were ever found. There was no way for a *human* killer to have escaped, either, so the workers packed their bags and moved!

The Equitable Gas Company was also responsible for the ultimate demise of the Congelier House. On November 14, 1927, a crew was fixing a leak atop a storage tank when a spark ignited it. The tank blew sky-high in a huge eruption that scattered debris and body parts for miles. Other tanks soon exploded, too, leveling the local neighborhood and injuring over 500 people. Twenty-seven others died in the tragedy.

The house the devil built sat two blocks from the blast site. When the smoke had cleared, only a crater remained in the ground. Satan got his due in the end. He took his mansion straight to hell wrapped in a thunderous fireball!

HOLY SEPULCHRE CEMETERY

Rochester, New York's Holy Sepulchre Cemetery dates back to 1871. It encompasses 332 acres and has over 100,000 burial plots. Some of the notable people buried there are silent film actress, Lois Brooks; Mayor of Rochester and Medal of Honor winner, Richard J. Curran; Major League pitcher, George Mogridge; and Francis Tumblety—a Jack the Ripper suspect!

The graveyard is home to numerous ghosts, as well. It seems that the children's section is especially haunted with small white apparitions appearing there regularly. Pinwheels decorating the grounds have also been known to spin like mad even when there is no wind. Cold spots are felt by visiting parents, too, while grieving the untimely deaths of their little ones.

The shadow figure of a forlorn young woman is spotted often during the twilight hours. She is thought to be Anna Schumacher who was decorating her father's grave when approached by a stranger. The man made advances toward the stunned seventeen year old that were instantly rebuked. In a fit of frustration, he strangled her, dragged her corpse into the woods, and buried her in a hole he gouged with a gravedigger's spade. The crime haunted him so much that he confessed to it in Philadelphia when arrested on a larceny charge four years later. He had brutally slain Anna on the bleak afternoon of August 7, 1909.

WATERFORD SHEEPMAN

In the 1970s, a biped creature terrorized the village of Waterford in Erie County Pennsylvania. The beast was covered with thick grey fur and stood seven feet tall. With curved horns topping its goat-like head, it trod along on hooves befitting any devil. Scarier yet, its hands were equipped with sharp claws instead of fingers. The creature's red eyes glowed in the dark or when it was incensed.

The Sheepman, as it was called, lived in a cave off Baghdad Road near an old sawmill. It raided nearby farm fields where it gorged on cattle that it tore to shreds with its canine teeth. The creature was sighted hundreds of times by spooked motorists and townsfolk.

The beast sometimes scared lovers who'd park on Old Kissing Bridge that spanned East Street. It would hide in the rafters of the roofed structure and leap down frothing and roaring. One such incident occurred when a carload of teens took refuge on the covered bridge during a rainstorm. The boys scrambled to put up the top on their Mustang while their dates sat shivering inside.

Guttural grunts signaled the arrival of the Sheepman who savagely attacked them. The stronger lad hammered the beast with his fists as his friend leaped behind the wheel to crank on the key. When the second dude dove into the Mustang, his assailant took out its fury on the car top. It slashed and mangled the vinyl with its claws until the vehicle kicked into gear. With his girlfriend's screams urging him on, the driver burned rubber off the bridge.

The teens' near escape spawned many more sightings in the next few months. By the late '70s, though, the creature suddenly disappeared. That seems quite logical if the Sheepman was an aberration who couldn't mate. A sheep, on the average, only lives to be ten years old.

BEEFEATERS

Before Beefeaters became a restaurant, the building served as the Carnegie Public Library in Bradford, Pennsylvania. Located at the corner of Corydon and Congress Streets, it served the community for ninety years. In 1991, however, the library no longer met the city's structural codes. After sitting vacant for two years, Dominick Cattone bought the property and established an eatery featuring beef on weck and a friendly ghost or two. When Todd Hennard took over as owner, a spike in paranormal activity followed.

Every employee questioned at Beefeaters has had a brush with the supernatural. Elizabeth Grohe, who's worked for both owners, believes that the basement is the most haunted place. When she first started as a waitress, she was required to wear a bowtie, a white shirt, black pants, and suspenders. Whenever she went downstairs to use the restroom, one side of her suspenders would come unhooked. Each time that happened, she'd see a flicker from the corner of her eye.

The kitchen is another paranormal hotspot where pans and utensils topple off shelves for no reason. Salena Hess was mopping the floor there by herself one night when ghostly fingers touched her back. Another time, she looked down from the dry storage room when she heard footsteps below. A shadow figure was leering up at her before vanishing like mist.

Lector, on the other hand, hears footsteps coming up the back hall toward the kitchen while he's preparing salads. He can't quite see the intruder, but he knows someone's there.

The lady bartender often feels like she's being watched. Although she's by herself a lot, she's not afraid. "I sense a friendly presence," she confides, "like a former librarian or children who come back to visit. I never see anyone but don't feel threatened at all."

Edward Johnson, the chef, agrees with this assessment. He was washing his hands in the upstairs restroom one evening when he felt a warm touch on his forearm. "It was like fingers encircled my wrist," he murmured. "Not in a bad way, but just to say, 'I'm here.'"

Tara Munch even views the spirits as playful and insists that they like to tease her. Recently, she placed a huge wreath over the fireplace after closing time. Although she checked it twice at home, it wouldn't light up when she plugged it in. She took it down, and it worked fine. Then she hung it up again only to have it malfunction. She removed it, replaced all the lightbulbs, but still it wouldn't work on the wall. Only after she yelled, "Stop it!" did the phantoms quit pranking her and allow the lights to shine.

Owner, Todd Hennard, doesn't believe in ghosts. As long as they don't disturb his staff, though, he's fine with their "presence." "Customers even inquire about them," he said with a wink. "I guess that's good for business."

WHISKEY HOLLOW

A five-mile road winds through bleak forests in Whiskey Hollow near Baldwinsville, New York. Satanists and the Ku Klux Klan used to worship there around blazing fires that magnified men's shadows and spit flames into the sky. The glens where they gathered became private little hells that shook with thunderous voices and the wails of innocent children. These babes were abducted along the way and served as a sacrifice to the prevailing dark powers.

At night, motorists still see barefoot kids limping along the Whiskey Hollow byway. Their pale, twisted faces glow in approaching headlights, and they often seem confused. Sometimes, they clutch bloody blankets in their hands. Before drivers can even gasp, the little ones vanish into the gloom.

USS THE SULLIVANS

The *USS The Sullivans* is a Fletcher class destroyer that was donated to the Buffalo, New York Naval Park after it was decommissioned in 1965. The ship was named after five brothers who refused to be separated when they enlisted during World War II. They subsequently died in tragic fashion.

The siblings served together on the light cruiser, *USS Juneau*, while it was engaged in the Battle of the Solomon Islands. On November 13, 1942, the *Juneau* was damaged by a Jap torpedo and forced to break off combat. Later, a direct hit tore through the ship's magazine. Frank, Joe, and Matt were killed in the explosion while the other Sullivans died after their vessel sank. Al drown a day later. George, however, went mad from grief and slipped from his life raft into a watery grave. The next time he resurfaced, he was haunting his family's namesake.

The USS The Sullivans had a glorious record of its own. It served with distinction in World War II, earning nine Battle Stars along the way. After an equally impressive showing in the Korean War, it was used as a training ship with the Sixth Fleet before finding a home in Buffalo.

Visitors to the destroyer these days are sometimes treated to more than just a history lesson as they often experience spooky phenomenon. Phones and cameras are known to malfunction while ship lights flicker and die. Balls of light are sighted on the vessel, too, and an apparition with a badly burned face evokes horror.

A memorial dedicated to the Sullivan Brothers is also a big attraction. It features a picture of the dashing lads dressed in their Navy pea coats. Interestingly, though, George is always out of focus in photos taken of the display. It is said that he roams the bowels of the ship searching for his bros. That well could account for the disembodied footsteps and sad moans echoing within the hull.

WHITEHAVEN CEMETERY

Established in 1865, Whitehaven Cemetery is located on Grand Island, New York. The tombstone of the little girl who haunts the Holiday Inn next door is located there. It's said to glow!

There is also the ghost of a woman who died of AIDs in the 1990s. She is seen often sitting on her gravestone holding her baby boy. A soldier killed in the Gulf War is present, too. He's said to be searching for his pregnant wife.

A local ghost hunter has identified seven different spirits that wander the graveyard. The only one he's seen, however, was wearing a tall hat. On his last daytrip to Whitehaven, an EVP told him to get out. His wife photographed a filmy object flying through the trees soon after.

Students from nearby Niagara University have had some eerie experiences after dark. As one lad lit a cigarette, he saw an orange orb appear above a young girl's grave. Horrified, he watched as the orb flew in circles and then shot underground. Two other students had a similar experience that scared them spitless. All three swear they would never return to the haunted boneyard under any circumstance!

DEAD MAN'S HOLLOW

Dead Man's Hollow is a 450 acre conservation area that stretches along the Youghiogheny River south of McKeesport, Pennsylvania. There are eight miles of hiking trails and the ruins of an old factory to explore. Other unusual features include the Table Rock, the Enchanted Staircase, and the ghosts of many accident and murder victims.

The hollow was once a major industrial complex. George Fleming's Stone Quarry, Bowman's Brickyard, and the Union Sewer Pipe Factory were all located within its confines. The Union plant manufactured clay sewer pipes for cities in Pennsylvania, New England, and New York State. It was built in the late 1800s and remained in operation until ravaged by fire in 1920.

Dead Man's Hollow got its name in 1874 when teenagers stumbled upon a corpse hanging by a noose in the eerie woods. The victim was never identified, and no one was charged in the murder. Another killing occurred in 1880 when George McClure was allegedly shot to death by the nineteen-year-old Ward McConkey. Ward continued to maintain his innocence until he was executed three years later. Some say his ghost has returned to the vale to seek out evidence needed to exonerate him.

Weird accidents have also produced phantoms in the gnarled forests of the hollow. In March of 1883, three quarry workers attempted to thaw out frozen dynamite by an open fire. They were ripped apart by the resulting blast. A worker at the pipe factory met a bizarre end, as well. On September 5, 1909, he was crushed in an elevator mishap and died on his way to the hospital.

The robbers of a nearby bank sought refuge in Dead Man's Hollow, and that ended badly, too. One of the thieves shot his accomplice, so he could have the money for himself. After stashing his loot, he was found by lawmen who gunned him down in turn. No one has located the cash to this day. Whenever treasure hunters get too close, they are pushed or tripped or sent packing by menacing voices.

Then there's the tale of the man who fell from a ferry and perished in the Youghiogheny River. His specter is said to come ashore and attempt to drag hikers into the water. They grapple with an unseen force until it loses its grip or is beaten back. Unlucky victims of the vengeful wraith are found floating downstream.

Another urban legend from Dead Man's Hollow involves an unidentified creature that slithers on its belly through the brush. First spotted in the 1860s, it was described as being forty to fifty feet long. Could it be a huge rattler that people have seen? Or an invented monster meant to keep snoopers from a criminal's lair?

WESTLINE BIGFOOT

Westline is located in McKean County Pennsylvania. It became a thriving village after Ralph Day built a chemical plant there in the late 1890s. To supply his factory with timber, he bought thousands of acres of woodland from Thundershower Run to the town of Guffy. The Day Chemical Company manufactured charcoal, wood alcohol, and acetic acid. Their products were shipped on the Kinzua Valley Railroad to the town of Kinzua. From there they were transported to city markets by the Pennsylvania Railroad line. All went well until the timber was exhausted in 1953. Then the factory was forced to close.

During Westline's heyday, it boasted a population of over 700 people. Among them was Shirley Stroup. Her father worked long hours as a logger, so it fell to her mother, Queen, to run the household and discipline the family's dozen children. The second task she was good at, and her kids jumped when she whistled.

One day in August of 1939, Queen armed her brood with buckets and said not to return until they were filled with plump blackberries. She wanted to bake pies and can berries for the coming winter. "Snap to it!" she barked as she shooed her girls out the door.

The kids trooped off into the slashing surrounding the village where blackberries grew in great profusion. Soon, they were surrounded by prickly bushes that grew higher than their heads. They heard stories of bears in the area, so they stuck close together as they worked away. With some berries being bigger than their thumbs, filling their pails was easy.

Their task was only about half done when Shirley heard a loud rattle on the other side of the bushes. She and her sisters edged away and picked a little quicker. They were more afraid of their mother's wrath than of what was feeding opposite them. No matter where they moved, however, the intruder seemed to follow. An unpleasant smell invaded their nostrils, too.

"What in the world?" gasped Shirley's older sister. "Whoever's over there must have forgotten to bathe this morning!"

The words were no sooner spoken when a giant, hairy man stood up and glowered down at them. He was way taller than the blackberry brambles, and the children didn't wait around for a second look. They didn't care what trouble awaited them, either, when they lit out for home.

Shirley always remembered the sighting of the strange man and spoke of it often. It wasn't until the 1967 Patterson-Gimlin footage of a suspected Bigfoot aired on television that she had anything to compare it to.

"Why, that's him!" she exclaimed, staring aghast at the TV screen. "That's who we saw all those years ago! Imagine having Bigfoot for a neighbor!"

OLMSTED MANOR

The Olmsted Manor is a Tudor style mansion located at 17 East Main Street in Ludlow, Pennsylvania. Its original owner, George Olmsted, made his fortune operating the J.G. Curtis Tannery and through organizing the Long Island Lighting Company. His latter firm provided power for most of Long Island, New York.

After Mr. Olmsted married Iva Catherine Groves in 1904, he needed a grand home for his growing family that included a son born in 1908 and a daughter conceived four years later. He enlisted famed architect, Albert Bodker of

Philadelphia, to design the dwelling and the Hyde-Murphy Company of Ridgway to build it.

The Olmsted Manor was completed in 1917. It was marvelous to behold with oak paneling, stained glass family crests, and even a two-lane bowling alley on the third floor. The surrounding grounds were also magnificent. They included sunken gardens, terraced flower gardens, and flowing fountains spewing spring water from the neighboring hillside. Mrs. Olmsted hired fourteen full-time gardeners to help her maintain the property.

In 1969, the Olmsted family bequeathed their estate to the Western Pennsylvania Conference of the United Methodist Church. The church, in turn, established an Adult Retreat and Renewal Center. The mission statement of the facility was "to provide sacred space for renewal in the atmosphere of Christian hospitality."

On one such retreat, a group of retired teachers were given a tour of Olmsted Manor. One of the ladies got some very spooky vibes when entering the bowling alley and fled back into the hall. Later, the party was descending the stairs, and the guests took photos of each other. The pics were examined only to discover numerous orbs surrounding the teacher with psychic abilities.

Another gentleman had a knee-high apparition standing next to him in his photo. He gasped in disbelief as he saw it, for earlier in the tour he learned that a child had died of smallpox in the house. The guide gave an evasive answer and immediately changed the subject when asked if the manor was haunted.

GREEN MAN OF PITTSBURGH

The Green Man of Pittsburgh was not a monster but an unfortunate human being. Raymond Robinson was his name, and he was the victim of a childhood dare. While he and his friends were on their way to a local swimming hole, they spotted a bird's nest nestled atop a girder carrying electrical wires over Harmony Bridge near Monaca, Pennsylvania.

"Bet ya won't climb up an' count the babies in that nest, Ray," challenged a surly boy.

"The chicken won't do it," heckled a second lad. "He's scared ta stand on a footstool."

"Oh, yeah?" sang eight-year-old Raymond. "Just watch me!"

Robinson scaled the girder like a monkey, but before completing his quest, made contact with a wire charged with 22,000 volts. He was twisted to and fro and then hurled back to the bridge deck. The electricity had melted his face, amputated his left arm below the elbow, and permanently blinded him. Only by a miracle did he survive after weeks of treatment in the Providence Hospital.

The accident left a hole where Ray's nose had been, burned off an ear, and made his skin glow green. Whenever he ventured out of the house, he was subjected to ridicule. Some parents told him to stay away, because he frightened their children. Others dubbed him "Charlie No-Face."

From then on, Ray only went out at night. Using a walking stick when he got older, he hiked along State Route 351 between Koppel and New Galilee. Passing motorists often stopped to have their picture taken with him. In return, they gave him cigarettes and beer. By the 1960s, cars caused traffic jams as gawkers packed the highway to get a glimpse of Charlie No-Face.

The Green Man myth has continued to snowball even after Robinson's death in 1985. It's mostly teenagers who keep it alive today. Often, they'll drive out to Piney Fork Tunnel in South Park Township that Ray supposedly haunts. After driving into the tunnel, they'll snap off their lights and call out to their glowing green hero. Once he appears, his electric-charged skin causes cars to stall or not even start once he touches a vehicle.

To discourage thrill seekers, the township now stores road salt in the old Pennsylvania Railroad tunnel. This strategy won't work much longer, though, for the underpass will soon be added to the Rails-to-Trails bike trail network. The Piney Fork Tunnel is located not far from where Raymond Robinson suffered his accident. His grave is near there, too, in Beaver Falls' Grandview Cemetery.

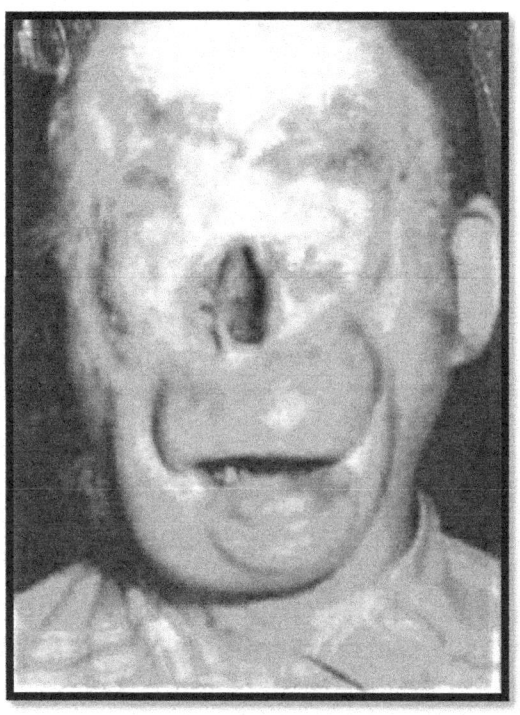

HESSEL GESSEL

James Hesselgessel founded one of the first stone quarries in Pennsylvania in the 1830s. James was a German immigrant, and his mine was situated on a hilltop near Asaph in Tioga County. He specialized in millstones and provided them to the Beach Mill at Little Marsh, PA; the Billings Mill at Knoxville, PA; and the Ainsley Mill at Galeton, PA.

James' business continued to flourish until he mysteriously disappeared in the 1860s during the Civil War. Some say he joined the Union Army and was killed in battle. Others insisted that the rival Shooting Star Masons murdered him and buried his remains in the woods. At any rate, he didn't return in human form—but as a ghost!

Visitors to the Hessel Gessel wilderness area today can still explore the rock outcroppings where the stone quarry was worked. Just beyond, there's a boulder field that's equally interesting. What are not so piquant are the ticks, timber rattlers, and poison ivy that one can encounter in the summer months.

Brushes with the supernatural are often experienced, too. They include disembodied footsteps that crash through the leaves and laughter that echoes from everywhere at once. There are also vehicle and equipment failures that can't be explained.

Adding to the horror are demons that guard the Indian burial grounds found at Hessel Gessel. They are known to push and scratch tourists to show they're not wanted. Others say that trees close in around their vehicles as they drive up the road. Dancing lights on a dried-up lake bed are another sign that Native American spirits reside here. According to legend, the Indians moved from the area because it was cursed.

Nighttime investigations can lead to other issues. A multitude of peepers reach an eerie crescendo in the spring while Indian ghosts imitate the howl of coyotes. Sudden temperature drops chill one to the bone, and handprints appear magically on Jeep windows. A deep voice then tells investigators to leave, and usually they do!

LEFTY

Antrim is located on Route 660 in Tioga County Pennsylvania a few miles south of Wellsboro. The town was built in the 1800s when coal was discovered in the region. The Annie F. Mine was one of its biggest producers.

A truck driver named Joe arrived early one morning at the Annie F. and had time to kill before his scheduled coal run. After parking his vehicle, he ventured into the mine to see some friends. He had barely descended into a restricted area in the dimly-lit shaft when a misty figure materialized from the gloom. It resembled a former foreman wrapped in a man-shaped cloud. While the driver stared in disbelief, the apparition shook a warning finger at him and advanced in a menacing manner.

Joe spun around and hit top speed in just a few strides. He had been quite the athlete at Wellsboro High School, so he quickly outdistanced his unearthly pursuer. When Joe burst back into the daylight, though, he made a dumb blunder. While racing along, he glanced back to see if the ghost was still behind him. That was when he slammed into a tree and shattered his left arm.

His fellow truckers, however, had a tough time swallowing Joe's ghostly explanation for his accident. They thought he concocted it to hide his own clumsiness. From then on, they nicknamed him "Lefty."

BELHURST CASTLE

Overlooking Seneca Lake, Belhurst Castle is an upscale resort located at 4069 West Lake Road in Geneva, New York. Belhurst is owned and operated by Duane and Deb Reeder, and its name means "beautiful forest." The property includes two restaurants, two ballrooms, a winery, and a luxurious spa. It was added to the National Registry of Historic Places in 1987.

The castle was originally built by socialite, Carrie M. Harron. She hired a crew of fifty men, and it took them four years to complete the Romanesque Revival style mansion. Many of the building materials were imported from Europe to add to its romantic look. Before it was completed in 1891, however, two workers were casualties of the project. One man went crazy while assembling the roof. The other fell to his death from the heights of the tower.

Mrs. Harron's most famous guest was a beautiful Italian opera singer named Isabella. To escape her cruel husband, she fled to Geneva with a lover known only as Spanish Don. The couple were quite happy at Belhurst until the singer's husband tracked them down. In a desperate effort to escape him, Don and Isabella slipped into the wine cellar and out a tunnel used during Prohibition to smuggle liquor into the castle speakeasy. Just before reaching the boat that awaited them, the tunnel came crashing down. The couple were killed instantly and buried beneath a pile of dirty rubble.

Soon after, a lady in white began roaming the lawn between Belhurst and Seneca Lake. She looked longingly up at the castle until someone approached her. Then she vanished into nothing while issuing a heavy sigh. Many supposed she was Isabella's ghost, who mourned the loss of her lover. This same apparition flies through windows or flits across the Billiard Room balcony.

The specter of Dick O'Brien is known to haunt Belhurst Castle, as well. Until his death in 1972, he was the head caretaker. Dick enjoyed pulling pranks in life and has continued that practice as a ghost. His jovial laughter often rings out as he flings stuff across the bar. He's also known to drape tablecloths around the chandeliers just for a cheap laugh. He likes to turn showers on and off in the guest rooms, too. To let everyone know he's still around, he's often seen sitting in his favorite chair wreathed in a cloud of cigar smoke.

Pregnant women have also suffered a few chills in the hotel. They'll hear loud children playing or screaming in the corridor, for example, but no one is there when they go out to shush them. Other times, soft lullabies float into their rooms in the middle of the night after everyone has gone to bed.

Guests have reported spooky happenings in several different locations. One man was having a quiet drink at the bar when someone whispered "Cornelius" in his ear. Whipping around, he found himself alone. He had been admiring the paintings on a nearby wall and gave them one last look as he rose in trepidation to leave. The closest portrait was of a man named Cornelius.

The Billiard Room is the most haunted place in the castle. While staying there one October, a woman suffered sleep paralysis. Her mother, meanwhile, felt jolts of electric shoot up and down her back. Things only got worse after breakfast when the "force" that had been plaguing them locked them out of their chamber.

A gentleman's stay in the Living Room was equally creepy. Something pressed down on his chest at midnight, pinning him to the bed. When it finally let go minutes later, a window came crashing down. After that, he still got no sleep, for footsteps paced back and forth on the floor above him. That seemed strange, because he was the only *registered* guest in the castle.

The staff at Belhurst has experienced supernatural events, too. One maid swore that her leg got grabbed when she went downstairs to the laundry room. She also said that a side room in the basement was haunted. No one could go in there without becoming short of breath. "It was like the air got sucked out of my lungs," she confided, "and I wasn't able to enter."

674 DERRICK ROAD

A family that had two young daughters and a much older boy lived at 674 Derrick Road in Derrick City, Pennsylvania during the 1970s. The girls had an imaginary playmate who wasn't! Actually, it was the ghost of a girl just their age. She once had a playhouse out back that was the exact duplicate of 674. Ignoring her mom's warnings, she took a box of matches out to her hideaway and caught herself on fire. She staggered screaming as far as the backdoor where flames consumed her.

The sisters often felt the phantom's presence but weren't afraid of her. That's because she joined right in with their games. She even liked playing with the brother's toys, too. One year for Christmas he got a football action figure that would kick the ball to you. The kicking continued even after he tired of the sport, for the ghost wanted to field more footballs.

During another Christmas, neighbors complimented the family on their beautiful decorations that they said stayed lit all night. That seemed peculiar considering that the father turned them off at bedtime. A similar situation occurred with the mother's alarm clock that she got that year for a gift. It went off at all hours of the night BEFORE she took it out of the box.

The brother was away at college most of the year. One weekend, he brought some friends home with him. Saturday morning at breakfast, the young men expressed surprise that his youngest sister spent all night in their room. The accused sister swore that she was sleeping in her own bed the whole time!

The girl ghost also had a habit of answering the phone when the family was away. Callers would wonder why someone picked up the receiver but did not speak into it. On several occasions, the family returned to find the receiver off the hook, dangling by its tan cord.

Eventually, the little girl's presence faded from the house after her parents passed away. It was thought that her people came and got her and led her to the other side. . .

MARK TWAIN MANOR

Mark Twain Manor, also known as the Gibson House, sits along Liberty Street in Jamestown, Pennsylvania. Dr. William Gibson built the Tuscan mansion in 1856. The square brick structure has a hipped roof and a central cupola, or belvedere. It's replete with distinctive bay windows and columns topped with a scroll design. The wood inlay flooring inside the house is beautiful, too, as is the fancy oak woodwork. Mark Twain Manor was added to the National Register of Historic Places in 1978.

Back in the day, Dr. Gibson was one of the five richest men in Pennsylvania. He made his fortune as a developer, founding the Jamestown

Banking Company in 1874. He also dabbled in local real estate and in railroad building. As part of his medical practice, he became a pioneer in the urinalysis field.

Gibson was a world traveler, too. On a voyage to the Middle East in 1867, he ran into famed author, Mark Twain. Twain later spoke in Sharon, Pennsylvania to promote his book, *The Innocents Abroad*. Afterward, he spent one night staying with the Gibsons. Apparently, Mark's manners weren't to Mrs. G.'s liking. When he showed up for breakfast in his pajamas, the lady refused to serve him until he returned upstairs to dress properly. Twain also took a few jabs at the doctor in his book although he didn't mention him by name. Despite the evident friction between them, the Gibsons' home was renamed in Twain's honor when it later became a restaurant.

The Mark Twain Manor is also known to house a few spooks. Now, that it's being managed by the Jamestown Historic Preservation Foundation, regular ghost tours are a staple at Halloween. A local paranormal group has done five investigations of the mansion, as well.

The most famous haunting involves a woman named Victoria. On her way to be married at the Gibson House, a thunderstorm spooked the horses that pulled her carriage. Wild-eyed, the beasts broke into a gallop and overturned the coach at a sharp bend in the road. Victoria was mangled horribly and died the same day. Although she wasn't wedded at the Gibson place, her soul still found its way there. The distinct scent of lavender shows she's present, and on stormy nights, she vents her wrath by slamming doors and rattling windows.

It's also thought that the original owner still inhabits his Italianate style home. "One voice I heard in the past here made me think it was Dr. Gibson," explained a prominent ghost hunter. "It sounded like the voice of an old man."

Other strange activities have been observed by visitors, volunteers, and staff members alike. A painted figure of a boy and girl moves from window to window on its own while a missing lantern from the Civil War era is seen often shining from the belvedere. Then there was the waitress who quit in the middle of her shift after seeing "something scary" lurch up the stairway toward her.

According to paranormal experts, over 100 EVPs have been recorded, and energy meters have spiked in many rooms. Music and disembodied voices have been heard on the top floor, as well. What freaked investigators out the most, though, was when a mattress bounced up and down while one of them was sitting on it. Could a ghostly child have caused the movement? Or Victoria wanting them to leave?

BROUGHTON SCHOOL

Before the Broughton School was built in Pittsburgh's South Park in 1929, people died violent deaths on the same ground during the 1791 Whiskey Rebellion. More blood was shed in the 1930s there when miners went on strike and staged a brutal riot. Although the outdated 1929 structure has now been closed since 2000, its abandoned halls are far from quiet!

The shuttered Broughton School is located on Brownsville Road Extension and is currently being leased by Don Wagner. From the first time he entered the building, Don has encountered spooky phenomenon. Often, he's heard children's voices and their disembodied footsteps rushing toward him. After seeing shadow figures actually "switch classes," he summoned several paranormal groups to investigate.

One group used infrared cameras to monitor dark hallways. In reviewing the film footage, doors were seen closing and opening on their own. Other investigators saw a ball begin moving in one of the classrooms and then roll in a straight line that none of them could duplicate. Also, in the teachers' lounge, a piece of wood propping up a table leg pulled free. It then skated across the floor with a hair-raising screech.

A former janitor named Bill lurks in the basement of Broughton School. He is hostile toward anyone who sits in his chair. He called one ghost hunter a "dick" when confronted by him. A boy's voice in the same location told investigators they were "retards."

Most "remaining" kids, however, aren't at all insolent. One visitor heard "Psst" whispered close to his ear like the specter simply wanted his attention. A little girl's voice on another occasion giggled and said, "Hello." One child begged, "Please don't leave me," as if desperately in need of a friend.

IROQUOIS WITCHES

According to the Iroquois, witches are supernatural evildoers. They can cause sickness, drought, storms, and even death. As followers of the Evil-Minded One, the first deed of an initiated witch is to kill a friend or family member by using black magic. Men, women, and children are all known to practice witchcraft.

The Iroquois believe there are two types of witches. The first just needs a thought or the cast of an evil eye to harm another. These witches are shape-shifters, too, who can change into common animals or even a demon bear. As a cat or dog, they might shadow their victim while plotting their next move. As a mountain lion or panther, though, they can actually injure their enemy.

Other witches use sorcery to work their mischief through objects or spells. They will sometimes implant their victim magically with a deer bone splinter or wooden needle. They also might hide a charm, or "otkan," near his house.

Witches are said to possess two types of light. One burns within the witch and shines through her mouth and nostrils when she breathes out at night. The other is the glowing sphere that's used while traveling called a "witch light" or "ga'hai." Once transformed into this glowing ball, she is impossible to harm, and sometimes her face is seen leering from inside. She will often exit her chimney in this form to embark on an evil errand.

To thwart a witch, one may only need to confront her and make her wickedness public. Witches work in secret and might be afraid of those they torment. Other times, one must spy on a witch to learn her intent. This may involve following her deep into the woods where she'll work her midnight magic over a low fire.

Some evil-doers become extremely powerful by aligning themselves with "spirit witches" who are already dead. The latter will provide its living counterpart with luck and money in return for gristly gifts. One old woman prepared children for burial in order to cut out their hearts. Afterward, she shot to the cemetery, dug into a sunken grave, and fed the harvested organs to her zombie witch friend. When her act was discovered by the medicine people, kerosene was poured into the grave at twilight and set ablaze. A horrible babbling mingled with orange and black smoke as the spirit witch headed for hell!

FORT HILL CEMETERY

Located at 19 Fort Street in Auburn, New York, Fort Hill Cemetery is built atop a prehistoric mound builders' site. These ancient people also had a ring fort there that experts believe is at least 1,500 years old. Later, the Cayuga Indian tribe constructed fortifications, too, and the earthworks of their Fort Allegan are still visible on the heights. Yes, and the heroes of a third civilization are buried atop the others. They include Myles Keogh, a captain killed at Little Bighorn; William H. Seward, Abraham Lincoln's Secretary of State; and Harriet Tubman, a former slave and conductor on the Underground Railroad.

Some believe that the highest elevation at the cemetery served as an observatory for ancient man. It's also where a tall obelisk was erected to honor John Logan, a Cayuga leader and orator. Logan had been friendly to the white man until his family was slaughtered by Virginia Long Knives in the 1774 Yellow Creek Massacre. While seeking his revenge, the chief fought furiously in Dunmore's War of that same year. At its conclusion, he delivered a speech that was admired by Thomas Jefferson, who included it in his book, *Notes on the State of Virginia*. The last line of "Logan's Lament" is etched in marble at the base of his memorial. It reads: "Who is there to mourn for Logan?"

Jane Rogers is another famous Auburn resident buried at Fort Hill Cemetery. For thirty-two years, she served as the Director of the Cayuga Asylum for Destitute Children. She treated her charges like her own sons and daughters until passing away in 1892. She was so beloved by the children that many who died early deaths asked to be buried around her. It is said that a girl ghost frequents the gravesite and is seen frequently around dusk. She isn't there to haunt anyone but to find a playmate.

Other visitors to the burial grounds report illusive shadows seen from the corner of an eye. They are thought to be Native Americans still at guard over their long gone village. Mysterious lights are observed, too, while the clopping of invisible horse hooves is heard on the graveyard lanes.

Another disturbing phenomenon occurs twice a year at Fort Hill Cemetery. It's the migration of crows that attracts demon birds from every direction. They perch in trees to squawk and caw as they wait for their flocks to assemble. Then they whirl away in a cloud of flapping wings to the Yucatan Peninsula where they breed all winter long. In the spring, they arrive again with strident voices and an evil glint in their eyes. It is believed that they first came to this "Hill of Crows" after feasting on corpses at nearby Owasco Lake. This ancient battlefield is known to the Iroquois as "Deagogaya"—the Place Where Men Are Killed.

SPECTER

When a family moved into their new home on Clinton Street in Salamanca, New York, they inherited a ghost that they named "Specter." He heckled them night and day and had his own unique personality. They quickly became aware of his various quirks.

One thing Specter couldn't stand was loud music. The younger brother would just crank up a Ratt or Van Halen album when all the knobs on his stereo would wheel counterclockwise on their own. After the volume had decreased to a barely audible level, the ghost would then whistle his favorite Jazz Age tune.

Specter also loved to snap on the attic light, so the boys would catch hell for it. They had their toys up there and a cool racetrack that they played with every night after school. Although they never left the light burning, their mother would come home from her waitress job to see it gleaming above her. Invariably, she blamed her sons for running up her electric bill.

The ghost had an eye for the ladies, too. The mother was still good looking well into her forties, and Specter was quick to notice. On the evening she moved into the house, he flicked on her bedside lamp to ogle her in her nighty. He put his hand on her chest and held her down until his lust was satisfied.

After her sons joined the Navy, the mother promptly sold her home to a rich cousin. He then turned it into a rental property. His first tenant was a beautiful, young woman with a perfect figure and long, shapely legs. Specter totally flipped when he saw her.

In the kitchen one morning, the gal got down on her hands and knees to scrub the floor. Before she could finish, she heard a silky voice purr, "Are you ready?" Glancing up, she spied a misty phantom leaning on the counter by the sink. He was six feet tall and dressed in a sharp suit. After leering at her for a few seconds, he was gone!

Two days later, the woman's brother moved in to "protect" her. He and some drinking buddies refinished the attic with the banging of hammers and the squeal of saws. After a week of this racket, they created quite the bachelor pad. Specter got even with the brother, though, by

75

repeatedly killing the light in his aquarium until all his fish croaked.

Another time, the brother came home in the middle of the day to fetch his lunchbox. He needed to take a wicked crap, too, so he hurried upstairs. He knew he was alone in the house, because his sister was at work. Bursting onto the second floor, he heard the cupboard door in the bathroom slam shut just before he entered. With a yelp, he spun around and flew down the steps. He left a brown streak up the sidewalk while sprinting for his car.

The bathroom was the scene of another scary incident. The gal stripped down, got in the shower, and turned on the hot water full blast. The lavatory was small and steamed up quickly. She took her time washing her shapely body and long, flowing hair. By the time she was through, her concerns had been washed down the drain with the soap suds. That was until she saw what a lewd finger had written on the fogged-up mirror. "Are you ready, *yet*?" read the note.

That time Specter had gone too far. The pretty nymph packed her bags the next day and in tears moved in with her mother. Her brother wanted to burn down the house and "roast Specter's ghost alive." He only backed down after his sister bribed him with a fifth of Jack Daniels.

HUNTING IN A HAUNTED FOREST

Public land in Pennsylvania shrinks more with each hunting season, and along with it, the amount of game available. Instead of getting frustrated by the lack of big bucks, an enterprising hunter should seek the more challenging adventures awaiting him in the Black Forest.

The trees in said woods have knothole eyes and stretched mouths that denote the unknown horror pervading the place. Bare limbs rattle like bones, too, and elusive owls create a chilling clamor. The wind has a particularly strident moan as if mimicking the cries of lost children.

Thickets hide furtive movements and eyes that brim with menace.

Monsters reside in the dark hemlocks, as well. Some, like the blowdown creature, will entangle its prey in its gnarled roots and then eat him from the toes up. The grizzly tree is even more ferocious. Its maw is always open and dripping with froth. Its breath alone will knock down an intruder at twenty paces.

A hunter should be equally vigilant for wardens, for the game commission has just placed a bag limit on supernatural beasts. To keep from exceeding one's quota, he should check the latest regulations now available online.

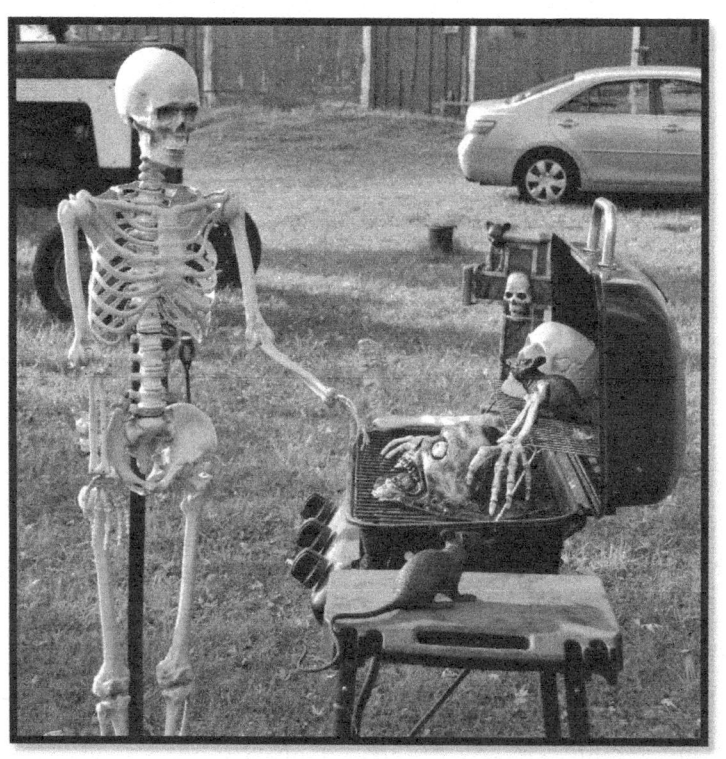

ABOUT THE AUTHOR

Hi, I'm Bill Robertson. I don't consider myself a spooky guy. I just like visiting haunted places and learning their history. I discovered the supernatural at an early age when my Swedish grandmother told me folktales about trolls and witches. She said that trolls would ride you to the ground and suck away your soul! My dad was extremely well-read, and he urged me in junior high to peruse the work of Edgar Allan Poe. I was especially impressed by the eerie settings Poe wove into his stories. It was the Gothic rock of the Doors, though, that hooked me on the horror genre. Their organ-mad music and tortured vocals had an irresistible appeal, as did Jim Morrison's dark imagery. To learn about my writing, visit **http://www.thehorrorhaven.com**.

BOOKS BY WILLIAM P. ROBERTSON

Short Story Collections

Lurking in Pennsylvania (2004), *Dark Haunted Day* (2006), Terror Time (2009), *The Dead of Winter* (2010), Season of Doom (2013), *Terror Time 2nd Edition* (2013), *Stories from the Olden Days* (2015), Misdeeds and Misadventures (2016), More Stories from the Olden Days (2017), Love That Burns (2017), War in the Colonies (2018), Fear Is Forever (2018), Fun in the Olden Days (2018), Come In (2019), Ghosts Revisited (2020), Ghosts Revisited 2 (2021), Ghosts Revisited 3 (2022), Ghosts Revisited 4 (2022), More War (2022).

Novels

Hayfoot, Strawfoot: The Bucktail Recruits (2002), The Bucktails' Shenandoah March (2002), *The Bucktails: Perils on the Peninsula* (2006), The Bucktails' Antietam Trials (2006), The Battling Bucktails at Fredericksburg (2006), *The Bucktails at the Devil's Den* (2007), *The Bucktails' Last Call* (2007), *Ambush in the Alleghenies* (2008), *Attack in the Alleghenies* (2010), *This Enchanted Land: The Saga of Dane Wulfdin* (2010), The Bucktail Brothers of the Fighting 149th (2011), The Bucktail Brothers: Brave Men's Blood (2012), *The 190th Bucktails: Catchin' Bobby Lee* (2014), *Annihilated in the Alleghenies* (2016), Ambush in *the Alleghenies 2nd Edition* (2021), *Annihilated in the Alleghenies 2nd Edition* (2022).

Videos

Ghosts (2020), *Gothic Poetry Slam* (2021), *Gothic Poetry Slam 2* (2021), *Gothic Poetry Slam 3* (2021).

Poetry Volumes

Burial Grounds (1977), *Gardez Au Froid* (1979), *Animal Comforts* (1981), *Life After Sex Life* (1983), *Waters Boil Bloody* (1990), *1066* (1992), *Hearse Verse* (1994), *The Illustrated Book of Ancient, Medieval & Fantasy Battle* Verse (1996), *Desolate Landscapes* (1997), *Bone Marrow Drive* (1997), *Ghosts of a Broken Heart* (2005), *Icicles* (2018), *Lost* (2018).

Audio Books

Gasp! (1999), *Until Death Do Impart* (2002), *Bucktail Tales* (2013).

Photo Books

*Tombstones & Shadows (2019), **Graveyards: Glorious & Ghostly* (2019), **Abandoned Dwellings* (2019), **The Pennsylvania Bucktails* (2019), **An Eye for the Eerie* (2019), **Ghosts* (2019), **Ghosts*

II (2020), **Ghosts III* (2020), *Serene Vistas* (2020), *Enter Winter* (2021).

E-Books

The above titles marked with a star (*) are also available in Kindle, iPad, and Nook e-book formats. *The Bucktail Brothers Series* combines both *The Bucktail Brothers of the Fighting 149th* and *The Bucktail Brothers: Brave Men's Blood* into one e-book.